W9-AAW-454

Let's Inves-Tigger-ate!

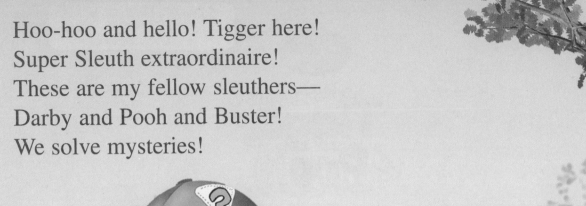

Hoo-hoo and hello! Tigger here!
Super Sleuth extraordinaire!
These are my fellow sleuthers—
Darby and Pooh and Buster!
We solve mysteries!

And here are Piglet and Rabbit and Eeyore
and Lumpy—and Kanga and Roo, too. We have fun
in the Hundred-Acre Wood—all year long!

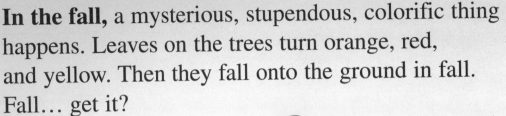

In the fall, a mysterious, stupendous, colorific thing
happens. Leaves on the trees turn orange, red,
and yellow. Then they fall onto the ground in fall.
Fall… get it?

Yoo-hoo! Calling all sleuthers!
Let's bounce and play in the leaves!
Hmmmm… Most mysterious…
Where could they be?
Look for the clues! Hoo-hoo!

The Super Sleuths are having a rootin'-tootin' party!
Yummy! Rabbit brought some munchy apples.
But ("Oh-my-oh-my-oh-my-goodness!" says Rabbit)
he doesn't know if he brought enough for everyone.

Think, think, think!
Can you solve this mystery for Rabbit?
Did he bring enough apples?

In winter, it gets brrrr-eezy
and snowy and sneezy!

Piglet says, "Pooh, I have a puzzle for you."

"A puzzle—for Pooh?" says Pooh.

"A poozle," says Piglet. "Raindrops keep plopping onto my nose. But when I look up… there's no cloud in the sky."

"Hmmm…" ponders Pooh. "That *is* a poozle."

That's a doozle of a poozle!
Can you sleuther-solve it?

Darby's in the middle of a muddle.
She has packed up gifts for her pals.
But her lids are all mixed-uppity!

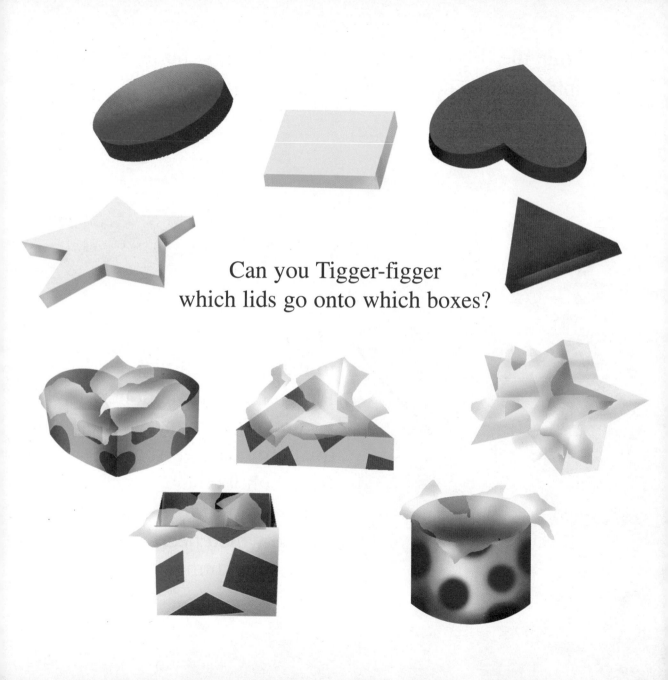

Can you Tigger-figger
which lids go onto which boxes?

In spring, the flowers are abloom with blues and reds and pink-a-doodle-doos—and Poohs! Hello, Pooh!

"Hello, Tigger," says Pooh.
"I was just saying please
to these buzzy little bees.
Please make some honey.
I want to say thank you to
the helpful flowers, too.
But… oh, bother…
I don't know which flower
helped which bee.
I'm rather stumped."

Let's inves-Tigger-ate!
Which bee came from which flower?

Rabbit plants new seeds in his garden every spring.
Lots of good stuff is gonna pop up!

"But, why does Rabbit's sign say **dots**?" asks Darby.
"Maybe he's growing polka-dots," says Roo.
"Maybe his carrots will have spots," says Pooh.

Take a peek from my per-spec-a-tive!
Can you figure out what
happened to Rabbit's sign?

Summer is a Tigger-riffic
time for lazing in the shade.
But there's always time
for sleuthin'!

What kind of clouds do you see?
Soft, wispy, whispery cirrus clouds?
Little gray nimbus rain clouds?
Or big, puffy cumulus clouds?

Pooh and crew see a butterfly,
a flower, a squirrel, and a honey pot, too.
Hoo-hoo-hoo! Do you?

Summertime is some humdinger-of-a-time to play.
But—uh, oh—what seems to be the problemo here?

"What can we do?" asks little Roo. "We have two short ropes. But we need one long rope so we can all play jump rope together."

Can you use your noodle
to think up a solution?

You did a super-duper job at
solving mysteries, fellow sleuther!
Thanks for helping me inves-Tigger-ate!